# Santa's Helper

Written by Grant S. Anderson
Illustrated by Sheldon Dawson

For all grandparents, both those here
and those here in spirit; our cauldrons of
wisdom, learning and love.

- *Grant S. Anderson*

It was December 23rd and all the preparations for the big night had been made. The school was completely decorated for this year's Christmas concert. Everyone had memorized their parts, and both classes of our two room school were ready for the show.

Miss Morris told us that almost everyone from the village and the parents from the farms would be there tonight, which could be as many as ninety or a hundred people!

Merry
Chri

"All right now, everyone take your places for one last run through before the concert tonight," called Miss Morris.

"Mary and Joseph take your places, shepherds and sheep, prepare for your entrance. You wise men just be patient and don't make any noise."

Miss Morris was in her first year of teaching and was doing her best to make this the greatest concert ever.

I quietly asked, “Miss Morris,” do I have to be a shepherd with Andrew?” He smells funny, never combs his hair, and I don’t think he brushes his teeth.”

“Sarah,” replied our teacher, “you could be a little kinder. All you have to do is walk on stage together. I could have asked you to take part in the square dance with him.”

**Yeeech!** The thought of dancing with Andrew made me feel sort of sick. Andrew’s family didn’t have a lot of money. He rarely got new clothes, why, he didn't even have a warm winter coat. Andrew didn’t have any friends and he really did smell bad. I guess walking on stage was better than dancing with him, and anyway, we wouldn’t have to get too close.

It was seven o'clock and the time for the Christmas concert had arrived. Even though some of the younger kids forgot a few of their lines, the people who crowded into our school didn't seem to mind. Miss Morris let us know how pleased she was, and that we should be proud of what we had done.

Following the concert, Santa arrived with a sack of gifts and handed them out to all the kids. Everyone received a gift except for Andrew, who just stood at the back against the wall, trying very hard not to be noticed. I had never really liked Andrew. I mean he was nice enough, I guess, but he didn't come out for recess and I had been told that sometimes he really did smell bad. But I didn't think Santa would leave him off the list just for that.

When we got home, I was still bothered by the fact that Andrew had not received a gift from Santa. He wasn't a bad kid. Was it that easy to be left off Santa's list? I thought I would ask my older sister. "You dummy," laughed Jessica, who was three years older. "That wasn't Santa Claus, there is no real Santa Claus. The parents at the concert bought those gifts and the guy in the suit just handed them out." I felt sick, no Santa? I couldn't believe it, what she was saying couldn't be true.

To be honest, I thought the Santa giving out the gifts looked like a friend of my dad's, Mister Francis, the man who ran the train depot. They certainly had the same laugh. I mean the real Santa had to be busy this time of year. It would be hard to get to all the Christmas parties all over the world. But to think there was no real Santa, I couldn't believe it, Jessie was just being mean.

I knew who to ask, my Granny. She would tell me the truth. I knew I could trust her and besides she made the best cinnamon buns in the whole world. I would go and see her tomorrow, right after breakfast. Jessie was so mean, there had to be a Santa Claus. Why would so many people say there was, if it wasn't true? I knew that Granny would tell me the truth. There had to be a Santa, where would all the presents come from? Granny would tell me the truth.

Granny had given me one of her wonderful cinnamon buns, and after getting about half way through it, I got up enough courage to ask her what I wanted to know. “Granny, Jessie told me something yesterday that I want to ask you about. She said that there is no such thing as Santa Claus, and that man last night was Mr. Francis, dressed up like Santa.”

Granny’s reply was swift. “I have heard the rumour that Santa doesn’t exist Sarah, and I hate it! I get more angry every time I hear people speak that way. It just refuses to go away. It really isn’t true. No Santa Claus, can you imagine that?”

I was relieved, but asked, "how do you know Granny?" "Why, it's simple my dear, I'll show you." She went to her purse, "here take this." She handed me a crisp ten-dollar bill and said, "now I want you to take that and buy a gift for someone, someone that might not get a Christmas present this year."

Who did I know that wouldn't get a Christmas gift? I thought for a minute. Why Andrew, of course. "Granny, the boy who sits across from me at school didn't get a present from Santa yesterday. He doesn't have a winter coat, so he doesn't come out to play with us at recess. I think I would like to get Andrew a coat, and maybe a toothbrush."

"That sounds like an excellent idea, Sarah, we'll walk down to the store and see what they have."

The store was warm and filled with the most amazing collection of things. Salt blocks for cattle, food for people, stove pipes, bolts of cloth, yarn, rope, twine, string, two bicycles, tools, shirts, boots, jackets, and coats. I found a red corduroy coat with a warm hood that looked like it would fit Andrew.

"Better get it at least one size larger," Granny advised, "he can wear a sweater until he grows into it." I also picked out a bright red toothbrush to hide in one of the pockets.

My uncle Arnie, who ran the store and post office with my aunt, asked me if these were Christmas presents. “Yes,” I replied, “they are for the boy who sits across from me in school. I don’t think he’ll be getting any presents for Christmas this year.”

He took the ten dollars and it worked out very well, because the coat and the toothbrush came to exactly ten dollars. I knew that when I didn’t get any change.

Granny and I took the coat home and wrapped it in paper with a ribbon and a big red bow. “Okay,”said Granny, after I had finished another cinnamon bun, “we still have work to do.”

We walked over to Andrew's house, between the grain elevator and the train depot, and waited in the bushes. "Go put the present on the steps, and knock on the door," instructed Granny. "Be careful, don't let anyone see you."

I ran up to the doorstep and laid the present down, knocked, and quickly ran back to where Granny was waiting in the moonlight. We hid and waited. Andrew's mother came to the door and found the gift. "We're finished here," whispered Granny "let's go home." "You mustn't let anyone know we've done this. Good deeds are best left untold."

I spent that night thinking about Christmas and what Granny and I had done. I still wasn't sure if Santa really existed or not, but I would know soon, tomorrow was Christmas. Would there be presents under the tree? Would our stockings be full? I thought mine would be, but sometimes Jessie was so mean, I doubted there would be anything for her.

Santa

Christmas morning came, and what Granny had told me was true, there were gifts for everyone. Our stockings were filled, even Jessica's. I wondered if Santa had stopped by Andrew's house? Granny assured me that he would have. We spent the rest of the day sharing our gifts and eating the huge Christmas dinner, which Granny had prepared.

It was January 2nd, and we all returned to school. At recess time, when I went out to the playing field, I noticed something I hadn't seen since it had gotten cold. It was Andrew, outside for recess. As I walked over to say hi, I thought Andrew wasn't so bad for a boy. I overheard one of the other kids asking Andrew what he had got for Christmas.

"This coat," he replied, "it's great." "Who gave it to you?" asked another boy. "My mom told me it came from Santa," replied Andrew. "Come on Andy," came a shout from another group of kids, "you can be on our team, give 'em the ball, lets play."

*I knew I'd be talking to Granny about this.*

"Granny," I began, "Andrew said that Santa gave him the coat." "That's right Sarah," she replied. I was puzzled "But you and I gave Andrew the coat. Doesn't that mean that there is no Santa?" "No dear," Granny disagreed, "we helped Santa with that one. You know how hard it must be for him to get everywhere, to visit everyone, all in one night. Santa can sometimes use a little help from all of us."

I was still thinking about this when Granny said, "there is one question I have." She handed me my second cinnamon bun and continued.

**"If there were no such thing as Santa Claus, how did you, my dear, manage to become one of his helpers?"**